PRINCESS GUSTY OX'S
STRANGE CHANGE

THE CRUNCHBONE CASTLE CHRONICLES

PRINCESS GUSTY OX'S STRANGE CHANGE

Karen Wallace
illustrated by Helen Flook

A & C Black • London

For the lovely Louise

First published 2006 by
A & C Black Publishers Ltd
38 Soho Square, London, W1D 3HB

www.acblack.com

Text copyright © 2006 Karen Wallace
Illustrations copyright © 2006 Helen Flook

ISBN 0-7136-7555-1
ISBN 978-0-7136-7555-9

A CIP catalogue for this book is available from the British Library.

A & C Black uses paper produced with elemental chlorine-free
pulp, harvested from managed sustained forests.

Printed and bound in Great Britain by Bookmarque Ltd, Croydon

Chapter One

Princess Gusty Ox stood by the edge
of the moat at Crunchbone Castle and
dangled a huge piece of rotten meat over
the green scummy water.

'Come on, sissies!' she yelled.

Nothing happened. Her pet crocodiles were hiding under the lily pads and nothing was going to tempt them out.

They hadn't always been so shy. In the beginning, Princess Gusty Ox had trained them to jump out of the water and catch the meat. Then she decided to grab one and see who could wrestle the other to the ground first.

It was a good game, and the odds were pretty even. Sometimes the crocodiles won and sometimes Princess Gusty Ox did. Prince Marvin, her twin brother, and her father, King Cudgel, often gambled on the outcome.

But no one gambled any more. There was no point. Now, the crocodiles always lost.

Princess Gusty Ox swung the meat lower over the water. She knew that the crocodiles must be hungry because she hadn't fed them for a week. Yet still the lily pads didn't wobble. So the princess pulled off her size-eleven boots and threw her pocket axe on the ground.

'Comin' to get ya!' she yelled and jumped into the moat.

Prince Marvin was practising riding a horse when he heard a dreadful thrashing sound coming from the moat. He felt sorry for the crocodiles. He knew what it

was like to have Princess Gusty Ox
wrestle you to the ground.

It really hurt!

Prince Marvin jumped down from the
wooden log that had been his horse and
peered through a hole in the hedge.

Princess Gusty Ox was in the water with
her arms and legs wrapped around two
terrified crocodiles. She was howling with
delight as the crocodiles rolled round and
round in the water, trying to shake her off.

Just then the Crunchbone Castle cook hit the tea gong.

BOING! BOING! BOING!

Prince Marvin watched in amazement as his sister bent her arms and legs and shoved both crocodiles back in the water. She jumped on their heads and landed with a terrific *thud* on the grass by the edge of the moat.

'See you later, suckers!' whooped Princess Gusty Ox. Then she grabbed her boots and her pocket axe and set off at full gallop into the castle.

As Princess Gusty Ox raced along the stone floor of the corridor, she noticed something extraordinary. It was so extraordinary she skidded to a stop and fell flat on her back.

The door to Crackle's study was open!

Princess Gusty Ox rubbed her eyes and looked again. Crackle was the court wizard and he always kept his door locked with a huge padlock and lots of chains, so no one could see how he made his magic spells.

In fact, Crackle's study was the most secret place in the whole of Crunchbone Castle and Princess Gusty Ox knew that this was the chance of a lifetime.

'I'll only *look*,' she said to herself. 'There's nothing wrong with that.'

But it was like looking into an Aladdin's cave! Princess Gusty Ox just *had* to go inside. And a moment later, she was standing in the middle of the room with her eyes out on stalks.

There were rows and rows of different-coloured pointy hats. There were shelves of potions that glowed in the shadows.

There were piles of dusty books and a rack of sparkly wands. But one thing in particular caught Princess Gusty Ox's eye.

In the corner of the room was a big oval mirror and she found herself walking towards it as if being pulled by a magnet. Princess Gusty Ox stared at the sign written underneath the mirror:

DANGER. MAGIC MIRROR. DO NOT LOOK. DO NOT ASK QUESTIONS.

'Huh,' muttered Princess Gusty Ox. 'No one tells me what to do!'

She took a deep breath and looked hard into the mirror. But all she saw was a wide face, lots of freckles, a broken front tooth when she smiled, two rather waggly ears, two popping-out eyes and a nose like a small, fat pickle with bumps on it.

'Huh!' muttered Princess Gusty Ox again. 'What's all the fuss about?'

Then a question came to her lips. It felt like something she had wanted to know all her life:

'Mirror, mirror on the wall! Who's the fairest princess of them all?'

'Not you, for a start,' said a nasty-sounding voice.

A rabbit appeared in the silvery glass. It had a mean look in its eye and its furry nose twitched as if there was a bad smell in the room.

'Call yourself a princess,' sneered the rabbit. 'You must be out of your tiny mind.' The rabbit scratched its ear. 'Haven't you read any fairy tales? Princesses are supposed to be sweet and pretty with dainty feet. They're supposed to sing high, twittery songs and bluebirds are meant to fly around their heads.'

The rabbit stared at her with its horrible pink eyes. 'They are not supposed to be big and fat and wear size-eleven boots.'

Poor Princess Gusty Ox! No one had ever talked to her like this. 'So who *is* the fairest princess of them all?' she asked in a miserable voice.

'Princess Lulu the Luscious,' said the rabbit immediately. 'And I'll show you why.' It began drumming its feet as picture after picture flashed onto the mirror.

The first one showed a beautiful, dark-haired princess wearing a glittering tiara and a frothy, white dress. There were pink satin slippers on her dainty feet and her teeth sparkled like diamonds behind her happy, curly smile. Her eyes were shiny green and her nose was tiny and perfectly formed. Princess Gusty Ox noticed immediately that it didn't look anything like a small, fat pickle.

There were more pictures to come. There was Princess Lulu doing all the things Princess Gusty Ox couldn't do. She was embroidering cushions. She was playing the lute. She was writing poetry. She was arranging flowers.

Last of all there was Princess Lulu
standing in a garden in a yellow dress
with puffy sleeves and a pink ribbon, and
bluebirds flying around her head.

Suddenly the mirror filled up with the
rabbit's mean, furry face. 'Get the picture,
Princess Gusty Ox?' it sneered. 'You're not
the fairest princess of them all! You're a
fat, good-for-nothing princess!' And with
that, it disappeared.

Chapter Two

'Is something wrong?' Prince Marvin asked Princess Gusty Ox. 'You haven't eaten anything.'

Prince Marvin couldn't believe it. The cook had made a slug and berry trifle especially for his sister, and she hadn't touched a mouthful. She hadn't even eaten a piece of black bread with mouse jam.

Usually she ate a whole loaf just for starters.

Not only that, she hadn't said a word since they'd sat down at the tea table.

Princess Gusty Ox looked up. After seeing those pictures of Princess Lulu the

Luscious, her world had been turned upside down. Before, she had been sure she was a proper princess. She could fight. She could chop down trees faster than anyone else. She could lift the drawbridge with her feet. She could wrestle crocodiles. There wasn't anything she didn't eat. Well, except worms, but Princess Gusty Ox was pretty sure no one ate worms.

Now she looked at Prince Marvin. 'Do you think you're a *proper* prince?' she asked in a small voice.

'Of course I do,' replied Prince Marvin.

'Do you think I'm a fat, good-for-nothing princess?'

Prince Marvin squirmed in his chair. There had been a time when he had called his sister 'elephant legs' and she had called him 'stink brain'. But those times were past.

'Of course you're not fat,' said Prince Marvin. 'And you can do all kinds of things.'

Princess Gusty Ox sniffed. 'The mean rabbit said I was a fat, good-for-nothing princess,' she mumbled.

'What mean rabbit?' asked Prince Marvin.

But before Princess Gusty Ox could reply, the door flew open and Quail, the king's trusty servant, walked into the room. 'Make way for His Majesty!' he shouted at the top of his voice.

A moment later, King Cudgel edged into the room. He was wearing turquoise-and-yellow striped pantaloons that were so puffed out and padded he had to walk sideways to get through the door.

Of course, the prince and princess knew their father was a snappy dresser, but today something was different. Instead of waving a fan or twirling a fancy walking stick, King Cudgel held a scroll of paper in his hand and his long, parsnip nose twitched with excitement.

'Dearest minors, mine!' he cried, helping himself to most of the sugar lumps that had been laid out for tea. 'I have a wonderful surprise for you!' He unrolled the scroll. 'I have invited visitors to stay! They'll be here in two weeks' time!'

Prince Marvin's eyes lit up. They didn't often have visitors at Crunchbone Castle. 'Who are they, father? Can we play with them?'

King Cudgel ruffled his son's fine, blond hair and swallowed another sugar lump. 'Of course you can!' He turned to Princess Gusty Ox, who hadn't looked up since her father had come into the room. 'Princess Lulu the Luscious will be a friend for both of you.'

Princess Gusty Ox felt her heart sink like a stone in a pond. 'Who?' she croaked.

'Princess Lulu the Luscious,' repeated King Cudgel. 'She will be coming with her grandmother, the Lady Hayseed, who used to go to embroidery classes with me.'

Suddenly Princess Gusty Ox jumped up from the table. 'Why didn't anyone teach me to do embroidery?' she bellowed at the top of her voice. Then she stomped out of the room and slammed the door shut so hard, it fell off its hinges.

King Cudgel, Prince Marvin and Quail stared at each other in stunned silence.

You could have heard an earwig sneeze.

∞

The next day, Quail was hanging out the king's vests after the weekly wash. This was normally the job of Mangle, the king's laundry maid. But since the king liked to change his clothes five times a day, including his vests, poor Mangle's hands had gone so soft with washing, she had been sent off to the sun to dry them out. As Quail picked up the last vest, he became aware of a rhythmic creaking sound.

Screech. Scrawch. Screech. Scrawch.

It was coming from the other side of the hedge and Quail was sure it was the sound of the swing. He put down the basket and peered through the leaves.

Sure enough, there was Princess Gusty Ox swinging back and forth, staring fixedly ahead, with her thumb in her mouth and a miserable look on her face. Quail frowned. Princess Gusty Ox had never sucked her thumb. Why on earth would she start now?

Quail knew the princess well enough to guess that it had something to do with her outburst in the nursery. No one could understand why she had been so upset. The only interest in a needle Princess Gusty Ox had ever shown was when she discovered it was the best thing to winkle out snails from their shells. Raw snails were one of the princess's favourite snacks.

Princess Gusty Ox sighed so deeply that Quail walked around the hedge and stood beside her. 'It's better to talk if something's worrying you,' he said, as if he was speaking to himself.

Screech. Scrawch. Screech. Scrawch.

Princess Gusty Ox swung back and forth and said nothing.

'Everyone needs some help sometimes,' said Quail, looking up at the trees. 'Even princesses.'

SCRUNCH. THUD.

Princess Gusty Ox dragged her heavy boots on the ground and brought the swing to a stop. 'The mean rabbit says I'm not a proper princess,' she blurted out. 'He says I'm a fat, good-for-nothing princess.' She glared at Quail. 'And don't ask me who the rabbit is because I'm not telling.'

'That's just as well because I'm not asking,' replied Quail. 'But if it's princesses you want to know about, I've got a very good book.'

'What kind of book?' demanded Princess Gusty Ox. She picked up Quail by his collar. 'Is it the sort of book Princess Lulu the Luscious might read?'

Quail nodded his head and made an odd choking noise, as if his neck was being squeezed and he couldn't breathe.

Princess Gusty Ox put him down. 'Then I want it!' She stamped her foot. 'NOW!'

Chapter Three

Ten minutes later, Quail came back with a checked wool rug over his arm, a box of the princess's favourite leaf-mould biscuits, a large mug of lemonade and a book called *How To Be A Princess – Hints and Tips and Lots, Lots More.*

'Here you are,' said Quail in his cheeriest voice. He spread out the rug, put down the lemonade and biscuits and handed Princess Gusty Ox the book. 'Now make yourself comfortable and have a read of this. And remember, everyone is here to help you.'

Princess Gusty Ox looked up. There were marks where tears had trickled down her greasy cheeks.

'I want to be like Princess Lulu the Luscious,' she gulped. 'Can you find me a yellow dress with puffy sleeves and a pink ribbon?'

Now it was Quail's turn to gulp. 'Of course, Princess Gusty Ox,' he said quickly. 'And we'll get you some white satin shoes, and I shall ask Crackle to train bluebirds to fly around your head.'

'How did you know?' Princess Gusty Ox's eyes were red-rimmed from crying.

'It's in all the fairy-tale books,' replied Quail. 'You never read them when you were little.'

Princess Gusty Ox looked at the heavy, blue book with pink edges that Quail had given her. 'Will this teach me everything that Princess Lulu the Luscious does?'

'Everything,' promised Quail. 'In two weeks, when they come to stay, you'll be just like her.' He looked into Princess Gusty Ox's miserable face. 'If you're sure you want to be.'

'I want to be a *proper* princess!' cried Princess Gusty Ox.

'There are lots of ways of being a *proper* princess,' said Quail, gently. 'You're every bit as good as Princess Lulu the Luscious. Just different.'

'I don't *want* to be different!' wailed Princess Gusty Ox, and she grabbed the book and threw herself on the ground.

'She said *what*?' asked Crackle, later.

'I've told you twice,' said Quail, crossly. He looked at Crackle's beady-eyed face. 'Now where would she have met a mean rabbit?'

Crackle chewed his lip. 'In my study,' he said at last. 'The rabbit lives in the Magic Mirror.' He frowned. 'She must have got in when I left the door open last week.'

Quail glared at him. 'You forgot to lock your study door? Oh, Crackle! Now what are we going to do?'

'Unfortunately, *I* can't do anything,' said Crackle. 'Princess Gusty Ox will have to work it out herself. She was the one who asked the Magic Mirror the question.'

'She's not under some spell is she?'

Crackle shook his head. 'No, she just did what she was told not to and now she has to put up with the consequences.' He scratched his ear. 'When did you say that Princess Lulu the Luscious was arriving?'

'In two weeks' time,' replied Quail.

Crackle's face lit up. 'In that case, what the princess needs is somewhere to practise what she's learned from that book you gave her.'

'What's wrong with the nursery?'

'Everything,' replied Crackle. He waved his hands in the air. 'No dressing table. Wrong lights. No decent mirror.' He gave Quail a cunning look. 'Don't you worry, Quail. Leave it to me!'

King Cudgel was standing in his bedroom room, looking out of the window.

A mysterious building had appeared in the garden that morning. It was pink and white, with lots of silvery bits stuck to it. PRINCESS GUSTY OX'S BEAUTY PARLOUR was written on the front.

'What's that?' bellowed King Cudgel at Quail. 'I want to know! *NOW!*'

Not for the first time Quail noticed a similarity between the princess and her father. 'Your Majesty,' he said slowly. 'You remember the moment the princess stomped out of the nursery?'

'Of course I do,' replied King Cudgel. 'Ever since, she's been acting like one of those wet princesses you read about in fairy tales.'

Quail cleared his throat. 'The thing is, sire, that's exactly what she *wants* to be.'

King Cudgel stared at him as if he'd gone mad. 'What?' He pointed at the pink and white thing in the garden. 'And how exactly is *that* supposed to help?'

Quail shuffled nervously from foot to foot. It was so unfair! Why did he always get shouted at for the things Crackle did? 'It's Crackle fault!' he blurted out.

'Then summon Crackle!' bellowed King Cudgel.

Ten minutes later, King Cudgel was sitting with his head in his hands stuffing sugar lumps in his mouth and listening in silence as Crackle explained how every little girl wanted to be a fairy-tale princess and Princess Gusty Ox was no different.

'But I don't understand!' cried King Cudgel. His eye strayed to the portrait of his dear wife, the great Queen Carrion, who'd been missing ever since she'd set off on a bear-hunting trip on her own.

'Her mother never wanted to be one of those queens in fairy tales.'

Even the *memory* of Queen Carrion and her terrible temper made Crackle nervous. 'You mean kind and lovely and always ready with the brimming goblet?' he gulped.

'Something like that,' muttered King Cudgel. He sighed. 'So what am I supposed to do about Princess Gusty Ox?'

'Tell her how beautiful she looks. *No matter what.*'

King Cudgel swallowed a whole handful of sugar lumps in one go and nodded.

∞

Prince Marvin sat in the corner of Princess Gusty Ox's beauty parlour and watched as his sister held up a cushion she had spent all night working on. 'Me First' was embroidered in different colours but it was a bit difficult to read because of the stringy pieces of knotted wool that hung down and the dark splotches of blood where she had pricked her finger with her needle.

'Well?' demanded Princess Gusty Ox. 'What do you think?'

Prince Marvin racked his brains. 'It looks very comfortable,' he said at last.

Princess Gusty Ox narrowed her eyes but said nothing.

She picked up a flute, held it to her mouth and blew. It sounded like a turkey caught in a mangle. 'How about *that*?' she asked.

'Groundbreaking,' replied Prince Marvin.

Princess Gusty Ox frowned. '*What*?' she said in a menacing voice.

'New and exciting,' said Prince Marvin, quickly.

Princess Gusty Ox thought for a moment. 'OK,' she said at last. She stood on a stool and began to read from a piece of paper. 'Here's my poem.' She bawled at the top of her voice:

'My love is like a red, red rose,
Because of his nose.
The more he blows,
The redder it goes.'

This time Prince Marvin was stuck. He didn't know what to say. It was the worst poem he'd ever heard.

Princess Gusty Ox held up her hand. 'It's all right,' she said kindly. 'You don't have to say anything. I know. It's brilliant.'

She stepped down from her stool and went into another room. 'Wait here and count to two hundred.' She looked over her shoulder and fixed him with a beady look. 'This is the *real* test and this time I want the truth.'

Prince Marvin felt his heart hammering his chest. He was terrified.

'Ready!' cried Princess Gusty Ox a few minutes later.

Prince Marvin walked into the room and thought he was going to faint.

Princess Gusty Ox was sitting in front of a mirror, looking at an open book and pulling out her eyebrows with a pair of tweezers.

Instead of her usual clothes, she was wearing a tight, yellow dress with puffy sleeves and a pink ribbon. Her hair was wrapped around strange roller things. Her eyes looked as if two spiders were sitting on them, and she had painted a strange black spot just beside her mouth. Her lips were red and her eyelids were bright blue. In fact, it seemed to Prince Marvin that the only thing that hadn't changed was her nose. It still looked like a small, fat pickle with bumps on it.

'Well,' said Princess Gusty Ox, in an odd, jittery voice. 'Do I look like a proper princess, or not?'

At that moment Quail rushed into the room. 'Princess Lulu the Luscious and her grandmother, the Lady Hayseed, are about to arrive,' he announced. 'The king commands your presence immediately.' Then he turned and ran so he didn't have to look at the terrible thing in the tight, yellow dress with the red lips and the bright-blue eyelids.

'Well?' said Princess Gusty Ox again. 'What do you think?'

'Uh, yeah, the thing is—' began Prince Marvin. He wanted to tell his sister to change back into her own clothes, wipe the paint off her face and brush her hair back into its usual haystack. He wanted her to know that he thought she was just as good a princess as he was a prince. Which is to say, not perfect. But so what?

Most of all, he wanted to tell her that she looked absolutely ridiculous.

But it was too late. Princess Gusty Ox stood up and smiled at her reflection in the mirror. 'I know what you were going to tell me, Marvin,' she said. 'I look like a proper princess for the very first time, don't I?'

Prince Marvin swallowed and admitted to himself that he was a coward. 'Yes,' he said.

Chapter Four

King Cudgel was wearing his favourite polka-dot tunic and in honour of his guests, he had put a bright-red ostrich feather in his hat. King Cudgel hadn't felt so nervous since the time Queen Carrion had asked him to dance and he had only been wearing thin leather slippers.

'Remember, sire,' hissed Crackle beside him. 'When you see Princess Gusty Ox, tell her she looks beautiful.'

Crackle fixed the king with a stern eye. '*No matter what!*'

'Are you telling me to lie?' asked King Cudgel.

'Yes, sire,' replied Crackle. 'And make sure it's a good one.'

The next moment, Princess Gusty Ox and Prince Marvin appeared at his side, and King Cudgel nearly fainted.

'What's wrong with my father?' asked Princess Gusty Ox. She looked at Crackle suspiciously. 'Don't I look like a proper princess?'

Crackle heaved King Cudgel to his feet. 'Tell her, sire,' he hissed in his ear.

'You look beautiful, my dear,' said King Cudgel in a strangled voice. As he spoke he met Prince Marvin's eye and he knew they were thinking exactly the same thing. 'Just like a *proper* princess.'

Princess Gusty Ox fiddled with her hair and a smile crawled around her cupid-bow, red lips. 'Thank you, daddy,' she said in the sweetest voice she could manage.

It sounded like a chicken scratching a blackboard with its beak and King Cudgel thought he was going to scream.

At that moment, the great white cart of Rosy Apple Manor rattled up the drive and stopped. Lady Hayseed climbed down followed by a pretty girl with dark hair and a serious face.

'King Cudgel!' cried Lady Hayseed. 'May I present Princess Lulu the Luscious?'

She turned to her granddaughter. 'And Lulu, this is Princess Gusty Ox and Prince Marvin.'

For a moment the three children stared at each other. No one knew what to say.

Prince Marvin was looking at Princess Lulu and thinking: Wow! She's *fantastic*!

Princess Lulu was looking at Princess Gusty Ox and thinking: Why has she covered her face in make-up and why is she wearing that *awful* dress?

Princess Gusty Ox was looking at Princess Lulu and thinking: How can she

look so pretty without wearing a tight
dress or any make-up?

'Run along and play, children,' said King
Cudgel, quickly.

'Yes, yes!' Lady Hayseed clapped her
hands. 'Go and make friends!'

∞

'What would you like to see first?' Prince
Marvin asked shyly. Princess Lulu was so
pretty he could hardly look at her.

'How about my embroidery?' said Princess Gusty Ox in her terrible, new sweet voice. She turned and smiled lopsidedly at Princess Lulu. 'Or would you prefer to hear me play my flute?'

Princess Lulu was puzzled. Her grandmother had promised her that Princess Gusty Ox wasn't like the boring princesses her mother usually made her play with. And now here she was asking her to do the very things she hated.

'Why don't we show Princess Lulu our trampoline?' said Prince Marvin quickly. The idea of making this lovely girl look at his sister's awful cushion or, worse, hear her music was too dreadful. 'We could even jump on it!'

'What!' squawked Princess Gusty Ox. 'That would be far too unladylike!'

But Princess Lulu's eyes lit up. 'I'd love to have a go!' she cried. 'I've never been on a trampoline.'

'What!' squawked Princess Gusty Ox again. 'You'll be wanting to swim in the moat next!' She stared at Princess Lulu. 'I thought you were a *proper* princess!'

A silence fell between them. Prince Marvin found he was holding his breath.

'That's what my mother wants me to be,' said Princess Lulu at last. 'She wants me to do embroidery and write poems and play stupid music.' She looked at them with big eyes. 'I'd rather climb trees and jump on trampolines and yes, Princess Gusty Ox, I'd *love* to swim in your moat.'

Princess Gusty Ox stared at Princess Lulu's flushed, unhappy face and her mind began to spin. Something was wrong. Princess Lulu was supposed to be a *proper* princess and here she was wanting to do all the things Princess Gusty Ox used to do before she spoke to the mean rabbit in the Magic Mirror.

'I don't understand,' said Princess Gusty Ox. 'What's stopping you?'

'My mother wants me to be what she calls a *proper* princess,' said Princess Lulu, sadly. 'And that means marrying Godric the Geek, too.'

There was another stunned silence. Princess Gusty Ox's blue-lidded eyes popped out of her head. 'Godric the Geek!' she cried. 'But he's —'

'The weediest twit ever,' said Princess Lulu. 'I know!' She stared at Prince Marvin and Princess Gusty Ox. 'It's too awful! Godric the Geek actually *likes* doing girly things like embroidery and writing poems. He's even trained bluebirds to fly around his head.' Princess Lulu rolled her eyes. 'That kind of stuff makes me sick!'

Princess Gusty Ox looked down at her silly dress and felt her ridiculous curls. Now she understood there was no such thing as a *proper* princess. She hadn't listened when Quail had told her and she knew even Prince Marvin had tried to do his best. She had made a complete fool of herself and it was her own fault for talking to the Magic Mirror. Then she noticed Princess Lulu and Prince Marvin were staring at her.

'Is something wrong?' asked Princess Lulu.

'You look a bit strange, sis,' said Prince Marvin.

Princess Gusty Ox wiped her mouth with her sleeve and pulled off the fake eyelashes that were tickling her eyeballs.

'I'll meet you at the trampoline in five minutes,' said Princess Gusty Ox, then she ran off without saying another word.

Chapter Five

Princess Gusty Ox pulled off her white satin shoes and hitched up her skirts. Then she took a running jump and landed with a great splash in the moat.

It was like being in a jacuzzi! All the crocodiles were so desperate to get away that the water churned and frothed and soon the princess's make-up was all washed away and her curls were ruined.

Princess Gusty Ox clambered out of the moat with her hair hanging like wet string from her head.

'*Yesss!*' she cried, punching the air with her fist. Then she ran up to the nursery, ripped off her silly, tight dress and climbed into her own clothes and her size-eleven boots. Last of all, she fixed her precious pocket axe to her belt and fastened it round her waist.

∞

Prince Marvin and Princess Lulu were having such a brilliant time jumping up and down that at first they didn't even notice Princess Gusty Ox standing by the trampoline.

'You look *amazing*!' shouted Princess Lulu the Luscious. 'What's that thing around your waist?'

'My pocket axe!' yelled Princess Gusty Ox. 'I use it to chop down trees and slice up dragon meat!'

'Will you teach me how to do that?' shouted Princess Lulu.

'Of course I will,' yelled Princess Gusty Ox. 'We'll go hunting tomorrow!'

'Yippee!' cried Princess Lulu at the top of her voice.

Prince Marvin bounced up and down, completely tongue-tied. He had never known someone who could look so beautiful. A great *whooshy* feeling washed over him. The air seemed to sparkle with diamonds. Birds seemed to sing like tiny, feathered angels. His heart began to beat to a new and wonderful rhythm.

Prince Marvin was in love and he felt absolutely marvellous!

∞

'So that's why I brought Princess Lulu to see you,' Lady Hayseed was saying to King Cudgel. 'The poor girl has never had any fun in her life, and if her mother gets her way and she marries that dreadful Godric creature, she never will.'

'Godric the Geek is the weediest twit in the kingdom,' agreed King Cudgel. 'What's more, he's rubbish at embroidery. She can't possibly get stuck with him.'

Suddenly the air was filled with yells and screams of delight.

King Cudgel walked over to the window. 'Sounds like they're playing on the trampoline.'

In the corner of the room, Quail could see that the Lady Hayseed was puzzled. 'If I might explain, your ladyship,' he said. 'A trampoline is something you bounce up and down on.'

'Gracious!' cried Lady Hayseed. She thought for a moment then her eyes gleamed. 'Does it by any chance make your tummy go all fizzy so you want to laugh all the time?'

'Why, yes,' replied Quail, slightly taken aback. 'I do believe it does!'

'Haven't you ever been on a trampoline?' King Cudgel asked Lady Hayseed.

'Have *you*?' she replied.

King Cudgel turned to Quail. '*Have* I?'

Quail shook his head.

'Are you quite sure, Quail?'

'Positive, sire.'

King Cudgel held out his arm to the Lady Hayseed. 'What do you say we have a go, Ethelberta?' he asked, grandly.

Crackle had never seen such a sight. The entire royal family, along with Princess Lulu and the Lady Hayseed, were jumping up and down on the trampoline, laughing their heads off.

'The Princess Gusty Ox seems to have recovered,' observed Quail, who stood behind an enormous tea trolley laden with cakes and biscuits and two sliced loaves of black bread and mouse jam.

'Indeed,' agreed Crackle. 'That was a nasty moment.' A cunning look flickered across the wizard's face. 'And have you noticed the change in Prince Marvin?'

Quail nodded. 'I smell a wedding barbecue.'

'Exactly.'

At that moment, there was a tremendous *crash* and Princess Gusty Ox landed beside them. Her hair was like a haystack and her knees were scabbed above her size-eleven boots. 'Princess Lulu is amazing,' she said breathlessly. 'She's my first real friend.'

'So you won't be needing that book I lent you any more,' said Quail, smiling.

Princess Gusty Ox smiled back. 'It's a load of old rubbish, isn't it?'

'Yes,' said Quail. 'But you had to find that out for yourself.'

Then Princess Gusty Ox turned to Crackle and took a deep breath. 'I have an apology to make—' she began.

Crackle shook his head. 'No you don't, Princess Gusty Ox. I should never have left my study door unlocked.'

Princess Gusty Ox chewed her lip. 'You know that nasty rabbit,' she said at last. 'Did it really mean it when it said I was a fat, good-for-nothing princess?'

'Do you think it was true when it said Princess Lulu was a *proper* princess?' replied Crackle.

Princess Gusty Ox thought hard. 'No,' she said at last. 'Everything was pack of lies and I should never have asked the question in the first place.'

'Clever girl!' cried Crackle. 'You've learned a lot today!'

'I think the princess deserves a reward, don't you?' said Quail.

'Most certainly,' replied Crackle.

He waved his magic wand and Princess Gusty Ox suddenly found herself soaring through the air!

The next moment, she landed with a *thump* on the trampoline.

She grabbed Princess Lulu's hand and the two of them bounced high over the trees and right over Crunchbone Castle.

Princess Gusty Ox turned to her new friend and let out a *whoop* of joy! She had never felt so happy in all of her life!